The Jacquelaesha Trilogy

Jacquelaesha Books #1 - #3

Experience the First Three Jacquelaesha Stories

I mean, there's *only* three

Because it's a trilogy

By Jacqueline Daytona

Copyright

Dedication

This book is dedicated to the HATERS who said I COULDN'T . Well I couldn't n't. Suck on that.

Special fuck you to Rylee, Lee, Liam, Madison, Natalie S. from 3rd period, Mr. D'Angelo, my dad's weird coworker Ashley, and Kendra (you know what you did).

Table of Contents

Jacquelaesha #1:

Jacquelaesha

Jacquelaesha twirled her luscious black locks into a luscious black messy bun that hung casually and lusciously from her, to be honest, normal head. It was the day of her Lady ceremony, the day where she was officially a woman, or lady, if you will, and the whole village buzzed with excitement. Everyone except Jacquelaesha herself, that is. For, as physically beautiful as she was, she was also beautiful in the head. I mean, not her external head, that was average, as I mentioned before. But her inside-head, or brain, if you will, was beautiful. In the sense that she was smart. Also, it was a lovely shade of grey-matter, if you were to look inside it. But that's not the point.

There was a knock on the door.

"Knock, knock," a voice said and opened the door. It was Blag, Jacquelaesha's best friend. Blag was wearing a crown of daisies over her stick-brown hair, which hung down like wet horse hair. She had already had her Lady ceremony last fall, but you might not have guessed it based on her pimply complexion and tiny boobs.

Still, that hadn't stopped Blag from obsessing over every eligible boy in town.

"So, tell me…. How excited are?" Blag squealed. Jacquelaesha's sapphire eyes rolled like the waves of the ocean.

"Not!" she harumphed, the silky pink sleeves of her gown ruffling in the air.

"But why?" Blag said, "The whole village is coming out to celebrate you. And after today you are allowed to marry. The boys will be after you."

"They already are after me!" Jacquelaesha slammed a fist, bouncing her boobs, which were big. Like real big knockers, I'm talking. Like make Tex Avery bulge his eyes out, ya know?

"Well, that's good! Now you can have your pick. Unlike me," Blag sighed, "Just remember not to pursue Terrance, please. Really Jacquelaesha, I'm begging of you, please don't take my man."

"I don't want anything to do with Terrance, or Jaketteth, or any of the young men of this village! Oh Blag, don't you see, there's more to life than marriage and village boys?"

As she spoke, Jacquelaesha's amethyst eyes glanced out the window at the mountains beyond, shimmering purple like the blooming petals of a violet in spring.

"No, I don't know what you're on about," Blag frowned a thin, pale lipped frown. Jacquelaesha sighed the sigh of a girl who had nothing but youth, beauty, family, community, and acclaim. She imagined she would be doomed to be misunderstood…. Forever.

"Okay. Well. You've been staring out that window for a while, so," Blag backed out of the room, "Remember to be at the village square in half an hour, or you'll miss the ceremony and you won't become a Lady."

"Won't become a Lady," Jacquelaesha muttered.

"Yup, that's what I said."

"If I miss the ceremony I won't become a Lady of the village. I won't be eligible for marriage. I'll be shunned by everyone, have no choice to but to venture beyond these walls."

"That's how our society works! Still bragging about that A in social studies, I see," Blag said, "Closing the door now."

With Blag gone, a wild thought entered Jacquelaesha's beautiful mind. The glint over her dark eyes was that of volcanic obsidian – glass forged from an eruption of the core of the Earth itself. She didn't have to go through with the Lady ceremony. She didn't have to bother stealing Terrance from Blag and settling into an average life like her plebian mother and father. All it would take was ….

. . .

. . . .

. . . .

. . . .

. . . .

. . . .

. . . .

. . . .

. . . .

. . . .

. . . .

. . . .

. . . .

. . . .

. . . .

.. . . .Leaving behind everything she had ever known.

With lightning speed Jacquelaesha changed into her comfortable boy clothes. (No one would actually mistake her for a boy, that would be gross, but she did look like a cool, hot girl, and that was a risk she was willing to take.)

And then she ran. Ran so far away.

Into the mountains, on her trusty horse, Girlboss, Jacquelaesha rode. The air was thick with pollen, with promise. The forest hummed with life. Life outside her village. A life no longer sheltered, where she could be accepted for the oddball genius she was. She didn't know what awaited her, but she had to believe it would be better than the village. *Blag would never have the balls to do this*, she told herself.

§§§

At sunset, Jacquelaesha was still in the forest. On Girlboss she ascended the first peak and could see the twinkling fires and thatched huts of her village in the distance. Vaguely she wondered what had become of things when she had not shown up. Had her father and mother worried? Had her sisters and brothers? She hadn't said goodbye to any of them, but that was their fault, for not understanding her. But now, as it grew dark and cold, she began to fear. *I need to seek shelter*, she realized. Blag would never have thought of that.

Trekking off the trail, she soon found a cave, and began to set up camp. Her slender frame fit perfectly in the crevice, and her super-strong but not-bulky muscles allowed her to easily gather wood for a fire. Fortunately, her years being smart and not worrying about boys meant she knew exactly which plants to forage, which wild herbs could be ground for spices, which small animals could most easily be efficiently killed, skinned, and had their carcasses harvested for meat. And how she could make a hearty but still-gourmet level meal with the ingredients at hand.

"Roasted shoulder-of-squirrel with chestnut and wild onion!" she announced to Girlboss. Even though Jacquelaesha had forsaken all traditional female roles, she could still cook, because cooking is cool and practical, unlike lame, boring things like sewing.

"Who needs your clothes to stay together when you've got a body like that?" said a tinny male voice. Jacquelaesha spun around, seething, even though she had been just thinking the exact same thing.

"Who said that?" she demanded.

"Wow, you're fiery," a man stepped from the trees, paunchy and greying at the temples. He had a crooked smirk on his face, ogling Jacquelaesha with his beady eyes.

"Stay back! I may look like a damsel in distress but I'm… not."

"Oh, you are feisty! Why don't you come here and let me keep you warm?"

"I built my own fire, thank you very much!" she said, and flung the freshly skinned fur of the squirrel at him, which was legitimately effective. The paunchy man howled in disgust. Jacquelaesha brandished a sword, steadying herself for a fight.

"Yorkel, you swine! Away from her at once!" a disembodied, deep, manly voice sounded through the dark forest. Jacquelaesha and the paunchy man swiveled to face it. Soon, it would be disembodied no more. It would be very, very bodied, because into the clearing burst an over-six-foot, big-pecs, square-jawed, man. He was dressed in dark traveler's clothes, like a rogue, and his dark wavy hair waved over his dark stubble.

"Dirkard," the paunchy man backed away, "I had no idea you…"

"I will always defend the innocent, the righteous, and the helpless, from the likes of you, Yorkel."

"And yet, you are the most wanted criminal in the empire!" Yorkel sneered.

"That's right," Dirkard said, "I may be a thief, often a murderer, renowned for my brutality, but I have my scruples, and when I see some guy talking to a strange girl I think is hot, that's where I draw the line! Now leave, and never bother this cool, hot chick again!"

With a sneer, Yorkel faded into the trees. Dirkard turned to Jacquelaesha and put his fingers through his hair, looking like Idris Elba, or maybe Timothée Chalamet, or Warren Beatty, or even Cary Grant. Whichever male celebrity you think is hot, given your age demographic and personal preferences.

"You didn't need to do that. I can take care of myself," she said.

"Oh? Didn't I?" he said. He cocked his head and gave her a warm smile.

"I may be young and hot, and I may have just spontaneously run away from home because I felt misunderstood and have never had to rely on my own skills out of necessity, but I can take care of myself," Jacquelaesha said. Still, she couldn't help being intrigued by this wanted criminal who had just defended her. She smiled and her eyes sparkled like emeralds that had been mined under apartheid South Africa by Elon Musk's father.

"Fair enough," Dirkard said, "But you don't know this mountain like I do. You'll run into all kinds of shit. You need to protect your neck."

Jacquelaesha rubbed her slim, white neck, arching it as she did and parting her red lips.

"Don't get the wrong idea," she said, "I don't care about boys."

"Do you care about……..." Dirkard leaned against a tree "Men?"

"Are you a man? Or an outlaw?" Jacquelaesha asked.

"Well, this is outlaw country," Dirkard said, "And you're in it, now that you're on this mountain."

"I can take whatever you've got," Jacquelaesha said, "I've met men like you before."

"Really? In your village?" Dirkard stepped closer. He smelled like musk. Jacquelaesha's knees buckled, but not because she liked him. Probably because she was dehydrated.

"Do you want some water?" Dirkard asked.

"No… yes…" Jacquelaesha said. And as he squirted water into her mouth she thought *Maybe boys aren't so bad.* Then she thought, *Blag would shit herself if she saw this.*

END

Jacquelaesha #2: Mean People House

A gust of wind blew Jacquelaesha's luscious black hair – black as the color of the sky, and of the mountain – over her grim yet conventionally attractive face. Girlboss whinnied, not wanting to go further, but Jacquelaesha pushed her beloved horse on. It was not fatigue or pain that stopped Girlboss, but fear. Fear like a knife across the flesh, which would be painful if it happened to you but you'd also probably be afraid, and the afraid part is what we're focusing on here. The air was heavy with fear, and weird forest things, because they were deep in the middle of the woods up a weird mountain. Owls hooted, crickets chirped creepily, and the wind sounded like moans as it blew through the trees, which were crooked, and also black like Jacquelaesha's hair. Everything was black, because it was night. Which in this case is ominous and not something that has happened every twelve hours since the Earth was formed 4 and half billion years ago.

But they had to press on. There was only one place to go now, and it happened to be their destination anyway: the estate of the Hauntman family, led by Count Duke Vladislav Thaddeus Zweevil Caucasian Hauntman himself. The Hauntmans were a reclusive clan, rarely seen and with a sinister reputation. Not the kind of people young girls would, or should, seek out, but Jacquelaesha had business with them. And, as established in the first story, Jacquelaesha was not like the other girls.

Dirkard she whispered into the night. He'd been missing a long time – and Count Hauntman was her last lead. If he turned out to be a dead end – pun earnestly and voraciously intended – she didn't know what she would do.

She rode through the trees and there it was: the Hauntman estate. The mansion was like a bad memory, like a meal that's been left to rot, like a person who has given up hope and so they live life automatically, letting their mind slip so they forget things, like their keys, and they come home but they don't have their keys and their roommate isn't home either, so they go to text someone but their phone's dead too, so they find a café where they can charge it but they have to buy something first, and it's too late in the day for coffee and tea doesn't really do it for them, and they don't like paying for things like water, so they figure they'll get some food, and they ask the barista what's good, and the barista says that the café makes really good cinnamon buns but of course they're out of cinnamon buns by now, it's the end of the day and it's their signature item, but they have some lunch/dinner fare, so the person orders a grilled cheese and it looks really good but ends up being too greasy with cheap cheese, and the bread is thick but kind of tough, and they're like *that's why I don't order food like this at cafes*, but if only they had remembered their keys they wouldn't be in this situation, because for once they have leftovers they're excited about at home, but they aren't at home, are they?

Jacquelaesha rapped on the mansion door and was greeted by an old woman. Middle-aged, really. But Jacquelaesha was young and had really good skin, so if you saw them next to each other the middle-aged woman would look, probably, fifteen years older. And since this is a third-person point of view story, that's just an objective fact about these characters, and not a petty manifestation of ego on the author's part.

"My name is Jacquelaesha Comeupwithalastnamelater," she said, boldly dismounting Girlboss, "I have business with your... husband? Father? Brother? Cous—"

"The Count Duke," the woman cut her off, rudely, "is not at home. You must leave here."

"I will wait for him. I've travelled far and have important business with Count Hauntman."

The woman sneered a sneer like a knife across flesh, and began to close the door, stopped only by Jacquelaesha's sword.

"I have come too far to be turned away," she said, "Please, I must speak the Count. It's a matter of.... *Love*."

Her voice softened as she thought of Dirkard, and her eyes, black as the creepy trees, stared into the distance.

The old woman shook her head, "Since you insist, I will abide, but rest assured you will find no love here. Not at Mean People House."

Jacquelaesha stepped into a grand, dimly lit and dilapidated hall. "Mean People House?"

"That is the name of this place, the Hauntmans' ancestral home," the old woman said.

"Why is it called that?"

"No reason, it's just a name. It may sound odd, but it's neutral. Like how someone can be named Dick Cox."

"I suppose," Jacquelaesha said. She looked around the hall at portraits of the Hauntman clan, all of them frowning in old-timey clothes, staring at her like the sound of nails on a chalkboard, irritating her yet commanding her attention, forcing her to look, perhaps whispering that they'll catch that shark, not for three thousand, but for ten she'll get the head, the tail, the whole damn thing. And sharks – sharks were like fishes, but with teeth. Teeth that cut like a knife across flesh.

Suddenly, a crash sounded like thunder. But it wasn't thunder. Was it a ghost? No – it was Girlboss, the horse who had walked inside with them kicking the wall because it was a horse. The old woman frowned.

"I'll have you know, young lady, that horses kicking the walls is not what's done around here," the old woman said, "Now, if you can please control your animal, I'll show you to your chamber."

Jacquelaesha thought to tell the old woman to fuck the fuck off and kick her in the shins for speaking about

Girlboss that way, but she decided against it. Better to play it savvy.

Jacquelaesha told Girlboss to use her inside hooves, then followed the old woman upstairs to a creepy ass bedroom.

"I'm Mrs. Schadenfreude," the old woman said, "I will be sure to alert the Count Duke of your presence when he arrives home."

✝✝✝

Jacquelaesha slept awfully, plagued by nightmares. The nightmares were like dreams, but scary ones where bad things happen. In them she wandered the halls of Mean People House, running from Mrs. Schadenfreude and a young man, who were ghosts but also vampires but also *also* they were zombies.

In the morning, she had breakfast with Mrs. Schadenfreude, who was rather curt and rude, and met some of the servants, all of whom seemed a bit nasty and vile. *The persons in this building are rather unkind,* thought Jacquelaesha. It wasn't until sunset that it was announced the Count Duke had returned, and she could see him now.

Jacquelaesha put on a long-sleeved purple blouse with big sleeves that was off-shoulder, and a black patent leather bodice that cinched her waist, matching black leather thigh-highs that laced up, and black pants that said MCR on them. The outfit both contrasted and accentuated her natural beauty, complimenting her body, yet signaling that she was a powerful and dangerous woman, one who wouldn't be afraid of any mysterious count. She asked

Girlboss, who was in the room taking up almost the entire space between the bed and the door, to wish her luck before she went to dinner.

Mrs. Schadenfreude showed her into the dining hall, where, at the head of the table, sat Count Duke Vladislav Thaddeus Zweevil Caucasian Hauntman. He was old, and gaunt, like a house that is decaying but not the decaying house she was actually in, a different house. He had a long, pointed face with a slim nose, powerful gray eyes, and long hair. If he were aged down fifty years he might look exactly like the young, ghost-vampire-zombie man in her dream. Probably nothing to read into.

"Ah, Ms. Comeupwithalastnamelater," he greeted her, "I'm so glad you are joining me for dinner. It's not often I have company."

"Jacquelaesha is fine," she said taking her seat, "I'm not one for formalities, Count Hauntman."

"It's Count Duke. You can be both, actually," he corrected, "But please, call me Zweevil."

"Oh, okay. If you're going with that one," she said, "I've come here seeking answers. Do you know anything of a man named Dirkard Dirkardneedsalastnametoo?"

Count Duke Hauntman tapped his plate, which she noticed was empty.

"Doesn't ring a bell. Is this a lover of yours?"

"Dirkard was the finest man I ever met. I know he had a reputation for murdering tons of people, but he never murdered me, and that's all I needed from him," she heard her voice cracking like glass that's shattering maybe because someone is doing that parlor trick where they sing really loud and high, not that she was singing at all, you get it. "He disappeared a year ago, and ever since then I've been seeking him. I will admit, Zweevil, you're my last hope."

The Count Duke smiled at her kindly, but also, sinisterly. She had to wonder: is he being kind, or sinister?

"I may have heard the name, now that you mention it," he said, "If you'll stay here at Mean People House a bit longer I may be able to assist you. I do hope you'll be comfortable."

"Yes. Thank you," Jacquelaesha agreed. She ate while Count Duke Hauntman talked about his family history while eating and drinking nothing. She learned that he and Mrs. Schadenfreude were the last of the Hauntman line.

"Mrs. Schadenfreude is a Hauntman?" Jacquelaesha asked.

"Yes, my daughter. She married a man named Rhineland Schadenfreude, but they had no children, and he has been dead many years."

"Dead?"

"Yes. Regular reasons." Count Hauntman stood, "Anyway I bid you goodnight Jacquelaesha. Please make yourself at home, though please remember that we are old-fashioned people who like ladies to be proper, and not to do things like let their horses run around inside of buildings."

Proper ladies. Jacquelaesha wanted to grab his hand and push it into his face over and over again while saying *stop hitting yourself, stop hitting yourself.* But she resisted. She would play by his rules until she could get to Dirkard.

She left, haunted by the man's presence, which was like a knife across flesh.

The next day Jacquelaesha was exploring the strange mansion. Mean People House was old and odd, full of stuff like weird statues, weird wallpaper, queer mirrors, gay chest-of-drawers, bisexual candelabras. It was all very Victorian, or maybe Edwardian, or Romantic, or Rococo. She noticed that in the portraits, all the men looked a bit like the Count Duke and all the women looked a bit like Mrs. Schadenfreude. Well, they were all related, so that was probably the normal reason for it. One picture was of Mrs. Schadenfreude in a wedding dress, but over the groom was a big red ex, and his eyes were scratched out, and a knife with blood drips was drawn at his chest, and a dick with hairy balls in his mouth.

She found the library, which was like a bad smell, in that it actually smelled bad, and the billiard room which was like if somebody made plans with you and didn't follow up until the last minute when they were already out, and they expected you to drag yourself off your couch and meet them an hour away when they might not even be there when you arrived because they went out with their cooler friends. That's not an emotion Jacquelaesha could relate to, because she was always the coolest friend, but you, the sad reader probably would. And it's objectively what the billiard room was like.

Jacquelaesha was beginning to consider leaving Mean People House when something struck her like a knife across flesh. It was a door, a horrible door that was open, leading to a darkness darker than most other darkness. Above the threshold it read HAUNTMAN FAMILY

CRYPT. The door gave her the most ominous feeling she had ever had in her life. Still, she had to go in. Don't argue with me on this.

The lantern light revealed the names of dead people and weird ass crosses. She paused over one that read RHINELAND SCHADENFREUDE, with a dick and hairy balls engraved under the name. What had he died of? Surely, something regular, like Count Hauntman said. What were normal ways to die? Disease, thought Jacquelaesha, old age. Falling off something maybe, as long as you weren't pushed. *Missing Dirkard.* She missed him so much. Her love for him ached like a sore joint if you have arthritis and the arthritis is acting up.

From under the tombstone, a skeleton hand shot up. Jacquelaesha screamed. She ran, but not away, further into the crypt, because her natural bravery instinctively pulled her towards danger. She shone the lantern around and suddenly, the skeleton of Rhineland Schadenfreude was in front of her. He unhinged its horrible skeleton jaw and let out a moan of a voice that was like a gasp of a whisper.

"Hey…" the ghoul croaked, "I… like… MCR… too."

"Oh," Jacquelaesha, who had not changed her pants since last night, said, "Cool."

"Yeah… I… actually…saw… them… back… in… the… early…aughts… at… a… basement…show… in… Elizabeth."

"Oh, wow yeah, must have been cool haha," she said, "So yeah I'd love to talk more but I'm def busy right now. Can I like, help you with any skeleton things?"

"No… yeah… totally… I… understand…I'm an old man… haha… also dead… could…. You… avenge my murder?"

Murder?! It hit her like a lightning flash or maybe a less cliché simile. She asked who did it.

"My… wife… Brandi…"

"Brandi who? You had two wives?"

"No… Brandi Schadenfreude… Neé Hauntman."

Jacquelaesha gasped. Could Mrs. Schadenfreude have murdered her husband?

"Alright. I will help you, but you have to help me. Do you know of a man named… Dirkard?"

The skeleton wheezed, "Yes… Dirkard… is…. Here… in the crypt…. He… is… not… dead… you… may…save… him… still…!"

That was all Jacquelaesha needed to bolt, dashing madly around the crypt crying for Dirkard. In the distance she heard Rhineland calling after her. What was he saying? Something like *the Hauntmans are undead monsters with all the powers of ghosts, vampires, and zombies combined and their only desire is to feast on the pain of the living*? It *sounded* like that, but it was probably something different. She'd keep an open mind about the situation.

Her lantern shone on some words engraved above a door. DIRKARD IMPRISONED HERE. She gasped. She wept to think of her Dirkard forced into such a vile place, and the tears down her flesh were like knives across flesh. She lunged to open the door but was stopped by two figures. It was Mrs. Schadenfreude and the Count. Actually, there were three figures – a servant was being gripped in Count Duke Hauntman's hand. She watched as he bit down on the servant's neck.

"Zweevil, no!" she cried, but it was too late. Count Hauntman's long hair covered his face, and when he looked up, he had grown young! He was exactly like the young man in her dreams. She had prophesized this in her mind, and honestly, she was pretty impressed with herself over it.

While Jacquelaesha was taking a moment to congratulate herself on predicting this without even knowing she was predicting it, Mrs. Schadenfreude said,

"You were trying to help my awful dead husband!" she screeched and she had fangs too!

"Yes, because you murdered him!" Jacquelaesha also screeched, "And now you both have harmed my Dirkard!"

"Ah yes, your precious Dirkard," said Count Duke Hauntman. He now a deep young-man voice instead of an old-man voice, and his long hair, previously giving off Christopher Lee as Saruman vibes was now giving off dude-in-a-band vibes. "You love him and yet... you cannot take your eyes off me."

It was true. He swooped in and cupped her chin. *Christ, Dad,* said Mrs. Schadenfreude. But they didn't pay attention to her. They were staring at each other, each of them enraptured with the other's presence, as if she were a knife and he was a magnetic strip you hang in your kitchen. But if the magnet is too powerful you can hurt your finger. They entwined their fingers. Would their fingers be hurt? Magnets were a mysterious thing. How did they work? Perhaps Count Hauntman, with his immortality, would know the answer. But maybe he would be dead soon instead of continuing to be immortal. Because she was a knife.

From her MCR pants pocket she pulled the wooden stake, which was also laced with anti-ghost and anti-zombie properties, and plunged it into his chest. He fell, staring at her, and whispered with his final breath, "Jacquelaesha… I thought you would be my spoon, but instead you are a knife. A knife across… my flesh."

Then he died.

Mrs. Schadenfreude shrieked and was about to attack when Girlboss kicked her in the head.

"Good girl, Girlboss!" Jacquelaesha hugged her horse. But there was no time to lose. With all her might she pried open the door to Dirkard's prison cell. Air of pain and misery wafted out of the tomb – yes, pain, and misery, but also of cologne, and drugstore strawberry body spray. There was another prisoner; they both looked up at her.

"Heeeeyyyy girlfriend," said Blag, moving her lips apart from Dirkard's, as he clutched her boob. Her tiny boob, Jacquelaesha might add.

"Huh. Didn't expect to see you," Dirkard said.

"Nice to see you!" Blag said. She pushed her out the cell and slammed the door shut.

The night mist was thick with despair as Jacquelaesha rode Girlboss down the mountain, taking one last look at that horrid mansion, her feelings forever hurt by the events of Mean People House.

END

Jacquelaesha #3: Jacquelaesha's Magic Triangle

The sun was yolky. The clouds were whipped creamy, and the sky was blue raspberry jolly ranchery. A perfect day for the start of the most auspicious event in all of the realm: King Henry James' Swinging Games®. Only held every $\log_{10} 100$ years, the Swinging Games® were the most physically, emotionally, and spiritually demanding competitions that anyone could imagine. The entire realm came out, sending their fiercest warriors to hopefully claim the crown. For, you see, these were no ordinary games: they were a big deal.

Jacquelaesha opened her eyes. The yolk was high in the sky. Then she remembered: today's the first day of the Swinging Games®! She grabbed her time pictorograph, which looked like, but isn't, a digital clock because they don't have those in this world. She yelped. She was late!

"Jacquelaesha! Did you just wake up?" asked a matronly voice in a condescending tone. It was Aunt Ethel, Jacquelaesha's guardian who, in both looks and actions, entirely resembled a wet cinnamon bun.

"Sorry!" Jacquelaesha moaned. Aunt Ethel had trained Jacquelaesha from birth to be the fiercest warrior in all the realm, despite the cinnamon bun thing. Winning the Swinging Games® was the most important thing in the world to her.

"Oh Jacquelaesha, you're so clumsy and awkward! Yet, I entirely expect you to win this intense physical challenge. The fate of all the realm hangs in the balance."

"I know! You've only told me a thousand times!" Jacquelaesha groaned. Aunt Ethel loved to tell the story of why it was so important for her to win the Games®. So, it's a character trait, and not bad world building, that she is about to recount that now:

"You see Jacquelaesha, King Henry James' Swinging Games® aren't *just* a competition among the elites to see who has the prowess to take home the crown. Years ago, the seven nobles of the realm, red, orange, yellow, green, blue, indigo, and violet, were placed with a terrible curse. Now, each of the realm's smaller realms suffers. Red is cursed to always have sirens going off. Orange is cursed to never be able to eat citrus. Yellow is cursed to never have good natural light in their houses. Green is cursed to be envious. Blue is cursed so that when each child turns eighteen they must choose between murdering their parents or killing themselves, and those who fail to make the choice bestow upon their entire family a pestilence of agonizing death. Their failure is marked by streams of black bile oozing out of every orifice as they rot from the inside. Many try to kill themselves then, but it is too late, they haven't the strength, and they die begging for forgiveness at their arrogance before the gods, to have thought that they could be spared the killing choice. Indigo is cursed to become cloying new age people. And violet… well, violet is us, and you know our curse Jacquelaesha."

She did. For Jacquelaesha, like all of the violet realm, was special. So special that they were shunned from the rest of society, outcasted, even though the violet realm *is* their entire society, but like, they don't all live in the same place. Even though the others do. The violets live everywhere else, where they are shunned for being too special.

"If only I could live a normal life," Jacquelaesha sighed.

"Yes. But we are burdened with being special. So special, that only a violet's winning the Games® can break the curse."

"Why doesn't King James just let a violet win? Or better yet, only let violets compete?" Jacquelaesha asked.

"He doesn't know about that part."

"What about the other realm nobles?"

"They don't know it either."

"Why don't you tell them?"

"I don't know everyone," Aunt Ethel snapped, "And contacting someone you don't know is so awkward. It really would make me feel uncomfortable."

Jacquelaesha nodded, because that made perfect sense. Boundaries are important. With that, she hurried to the stables to mount her trusty horse Girlboss. Her lavender and plum hair cascaded down her back and framed the large, periwinkle eyes that were the defining feature of her heart-shaped face. Besides her cut-like-glass cheekbones. And classically petite white-person nose. And full feminine lips. Also her tits were nice.

Speaking of, her frame was draped in a gossamer dress that shimmered all the colors of the rainbow no homo. People always dressed in the color of their realms, but since violets were special, they could wear whatever they wanted.

Jacquelaesha and Girlboss sped through the crowds to the Gaming Center, the giant colosseum at the center of the capital, to report for the Games®. Athletes and soldiers wearing armor of all colors congested around her, brandishing broad swords, daggers, throwing stars, nunchucks, tasers. Jacquelaesha herself was armed to the teeth under the skin-tight, butterfly-wing thin folds of her gossamer evening gown. But she was so well trained in concealing weapons that she could do that.

They arrived at the stadium and Jacquelaesha was assigned her place amongst the competitors. They stood in rows, waiting for King James to give his commencement. Next to Jacquelaesha, a tall, orange-haired woman smirked at her. Men usually liked women on the blonde to red hair spectrum, and Jacquelaesha bet this lady was used to getting guys. Even if she was a little too tall. And thin in a no-junk-in-the-trunk way.

"Well, well, well," the woman said, "I didn't expect to see a violet in this game."

"Please Cynthia. That isn't nice," said a man in yellow next to her.

"Wellity wellity well," Cynthia said, "Rubio is defending the violet. Too bad I'll make short work of both of you during the competition."

Jacquelaesha pulled out a dagger and held it to Cynthia's throat, "I'll slit your jugular open and pull out your vocal chords if you say one more word you ugly, emaciated bitch!"

Cynthia was humiliated and Jacquelaesha had impressed the crowd with her wit and skill. Everyone clapped!

"Wow, no one's ever stood up to Cynthia before. I'm Rubio," the man said. He had a chiseled jaw and tight, muscle clenching armor, with bouncing yellow hair that perfectly contrasted Jacquelaesha's lavender locks. Rubio is Spanish for Blonde Guy, so I basically have a POC main love interest even though he's by definition blonde and I will never explicitly describe non-white physical traits or code him as Latino in any capacity just give me the credit. Give me the credit. I'm white. Give it to me. I'm white, and it's hard. It's hard and I don't have a job. And I'm white.

Jacquelaesha couldn't believe this man was talking to her.

"You- you're – n-n-not a-a-a-afraid of m-me? B-because I'm a v- a v- a v—"

"A violet? No," said Rubio, bending down to gently kiss her hand, "I don't believe in that kind of malarky."

Jacquelaesha flushed. He was so handsome and polite, it was hard to imagine that she would have to fight him in the competition.

Just then the trumpets blared and the king appeared before the crowd.

"Hello! Welcome all to King Henry James' Swinging Games: A Good Time For the Whole Realm®," King James said, "We're going to have a lot of fun this summer. As a reminder, Swinging Games® official tumblers are back in stock. Keep your beverages hot or cold for longer with patented King James insulation technology. And of course, we have all the usual merch.

This is a special occasion: the 100th Swinging Games®! A hundred games since the curses that afflict our great realm were cast. They don't affect me personally because as the king I'm not in one of the color realms, but lead all of you as your rainbow leader no homo. For any extremely young children or amnesiacs who might be in the audience, a reminder that our world is made up of seven realms each magically imbued with the power of a color, and that magic is centralized in the power of the king, who rules the greater realm. None of us know why the curses happened, but we know that whoever is crowned the winner of the Games® has a chance to break them. It hasn't worked so far, but probably will soon. Maybe this year, with the 100th games.

But look, you guys know this already! And even if the curses aren't broken, it's still a milestone worth celebrating. You won't want to leave the capital without a limited edition 100th Swinging Games® tee shirt, hat, key chain, tumbler, or stuffed bear."

With that, King Henry James declared the 100th King Henry James' Swinging Games: A Good Time For the Whole Realm® begun!

"Up first," said the king, "Arnold and Tracy."

Two people stepped forward: a green man and indigo woman. They fought each other. The crowd cheered. *So much violence*, thought Jacquelaesha. The green man collapsed. He was dead. Yes, the Games® were a fight alright. A fight…. To the death.

That night, Jacquelaesha was holding her tray in the dining hall when she saw Rubio waving at her. She would sit with him, she decided, but right before she got to his table, Cynthia appeared. She was flanked by two cronies, a red woman and the indigo, Tracy.

"Where do you think you're going, violet?" Cynthia sneered.

"Um. My name is Jacquelaesha."

"We don't care," said Tracy the indigo girl, "You're not good enough to sit with us and Rubio. Your aura is all wrong and you have not aligned your chakras."

"WHAT DID YOU SAY TRACE?" shouted the red woman.

"You're a violet, and you're not good enough to sit with us," said Cynthia.

"Wow," Jacquelaesha, "Are you actually a green? Because you're just jealous."

Cynthia and Tracy made OMG faces.

"DID SHE SAY JELLO?" the red woman said, "SORRY MY TINNITUS IS ACTING —"

"How DARE you!" Cynthia gagged.

"Eat a lime, Cynthia," Jacquelaesha said, then turned around, swinging her perfectly proportioned hips.

"—JUST THERE'S NO SIRENS HERE AND –"

"Irene shut up!" Tracy said, "Cynthia is crying and it's hard on me, as an empath."

Behind them, Rubio waved sadly to Jacquelaesha, watching her go. He was a nice guy, but maybe too nice. After all, he didn't have the chutzpah to stand up to Cynthia and her mean girl clique. Jacquelaesha sighed, trying to find a place to eat. She passed Arnold, the green man from the first fight. He was eating a ton — he had to after being raised by the undead mages. Oh yeah, it *is* a fight to the death, but the King has magic that allows people to be brought back to life with no consequences.

There. In a shadowy corner of the cafeteria. A man put a strand of dark, shimmering blue hair behind his ear. He was reading a large and intimidating tome, sipping a tall mug of mead. He also had a chiseled jaw, and a visible six-pack, because his armor left his abdomen exposed.

"Can't find a place to sit?" an unfortunately familiar voice said. Jacquelaesha spun around to see the unwelcome faces of two fellow violets.

"*No.* I have a place to sit," she said, because like George Costanza, she knew these so-called friends were trying to stick it to her.

"Jacquelaesha. You can sit with us if you want. Look, Blag and I are really sorry," Dirkard said.

"Yeah. I mean," Blag sighed, "You and Dirkard had broken up, we didn't think you still had feelings, or that you thought you and he were still –"

"Talk to the hand!" Jacquelaesha said and put her hand up. So that they could talk to it. "I'm looking forward to beating you both and winning the Games® crown for myself."

"That's fair, that's fair," Dirkard said.

"I'm not even competing," said Blag.

"And I'm just here to kill people with no repercussions. Dr. Rubenstein-Carr says it will help me channel my aggression appropriately."

But Jacquelaesha didn't care. "Look, I have friends. I'm sitting over there," she pointed at the mysterious blue stranger.

"Him?" Blag clucked her tongue, "I hear he's bad news Jacquelaesha."

"No *you're* bad news," Jacquelaesha said. That sent Blag and Dirkard packing, with looks of resignation at Jacquelaesha's wit and certainly not looks of concern and mild pity. Still, she hesitated to go over to the stranger herself. There *was* something intimidating about him.

"Oh Girlboss!" Jacquelaesha said, eating her dinner in the stable, "What a day!"

╫╫

The next day Jacquelaesha opened her eyes and remembered it was the second day of the Swinging Games®. And she was late again! What a relatable trait.

Unfortunately, Jacquelaesha was sorted next to Cynthia and her posse again. Fortunately, that also included Rubio.

"Good morning Jacquelaesha," Rubio said, "I missed you at dinner. But, I'm glad you were late because I got to see you ride in on that beautiful horse of yours. What's her name?"

"Girlboss," Jacquelaesha said. Anyone who liked her pet had points in her book. What a common feeling that the reader, who is statistically likely to also have a pet, will share.

"Wow!" Rubio said, "What a great name. You must really be a feminist who cares about women's empowerment."

Just then, Cynthia, who was too tall and too skinny began shrieking in a shrill, nagging tone.

"Stay away from my man! I hate you, you naturally attractive bitch! I have to wear make-up but you don't!"

"Whoa. Cynthia, please," said Rubio, "You're being irrational."

"He's not your man!" Jacquelaesha took out a whip, cracked it around Cynthia's wrist, pulled her close, and head-butted her into the ground. Rubio rubbed his fingers nervously. Tracy and Irene rushed to help the orange woman up.

"Oh, you've done it this time violet," Cynthia cackled, "Oh I'll get you. Just you wait. I killed ten strong warriors yesterday, and we're about to paired up."

Just then the King announced the next to fight.

"Jacquelaesha and…."

Cynthia was smiling evilly. Her minions were cracking devilish grins. Rubio looked concerned for Jacquelaesha's fate.

"… Gloomithy!"

Who? Jacquelaesha stepped warily into the ring. The person who stepped out from the crowd was a man. A blue man. A mysterious, tall, taut-muscled, dark-glowering man who read ancient tomes alone in the cafeterias of magical castles.

Gloomithy. She thought. They approached, ready to shake hands as was the custom.

"Nice to meet you," he said, with a dark chuckle, "My name is Lord Gloomithy Bleaker, of the blue realm."

"B-blue r-realm?" Jacquelaesha said. She was nervous. Blues had a bit of reputation, since the curse which forced them to break the sacred connection between a parent and child or suffer unspeakable loss made them a bit much sometimes.

"Yes. And you. You're… violet."

"You may think me an outcast, but we'll see who wins this battle," Jacquelaesha said.

"You can be an outcast and still win, those aren't mutually exclusive."

Ugh, he was so rude. She was looking forward to beating him. From out of the leg of her silver latex body suit, she pulled a shuriken and hurled it at him. He caught it with two fingers, and his eyes were covered by that anime shadow as he cracked a grin.

"We haven't begun yet Ms. Comeupwithalastnamelater," he said.

"There are no rules in the Swinging Games®, Lord Bleaker. Only winners."

"Lord Bleaker is my father's name, and his father and his, all the way back to the original blue noble who was cursed. Most call me Gloomithy. But to some I am simply, Gloom."

"Very well, Gloom," Jacquelaesha said. After all, people named Timothy are called Tim, so it made sense that someone with the normal name of Gloomithy would naturally shorten that to

Gloom, and if that reminds you of a common noun meaning darkness or depression, well, that's on you.

They battled, and they both looked super hot doing it. But at the end, Jacquelaesha bested him. The crowd was shouting "Finish him! Finish him!" Her blade was at his stubbled throat. She… she couldn't. She put her blade down.

"What is this insolence?!" shouted King Henry James.

"I — I c-can't," Jacquelaesha, "Y-your m-m-majesty. This is wrong. We cannot fight curses with bloodshed."

The crowd booed.

"Silence! Silence!" King James shouted, "No one in the centuries of this tradition has ever made that point before. Young lady, you are of the violet realm and therefore an outcast. Yet, you speak the truth. You are allowed to spare young Gloomithy… for now. I must retire to my chamber to ponder this philosophical quandary. But in the meantime, the Swinging Games® shall continue uninterrupted! And to all you other competitors, who may be unnerved by this turn of events, I remind you that Swinging Games® participants are entitled to 15% off at official Games® stores. A Good Time For the Whole Realm."

Jacquelaesha couldn't believe it. She turned to say something to Gloom, but he was gone.

"Gloom!" she shouted. But he was lost in the crowd of competitors, most of whom were advancing on Jacquelaesha. Some thought her a hero, some a villain. Suddenly, Rubio's yellow hair was before her. He dressed in mustard and bright daffodil. His face seemed to glow gold, and his perfectly straight teeth beamed yellow. He was as light as the yolky day.

"Wow. My mind has never been blown like that," Rubio said, "You have such depth, as well as beauty and grace. Brave and strong enough to best Lord Bleaker, yet compassionate enough to advocate for his life. You have such contrasts to you, Jacquelaesha, like you are slim enough to pull off a latex body suit, yet are still well endowed in the chest and hip areas."

Jacquelaesha blushed. Just then, she was faced with the Mean Trio. (It was a working title.)

"You've ruined everything, violet girl!" Cynthia shouted. "I'm going to end you!"

She unsheathed her blade and leapt, but Jacquelaesha dodged and got her in a headlock. She dug her nails into Cynthia's head, pushed her face into the dirt and pressed hard enough that she genuinely began to suffocate. As her body convulsed, Jacquelaesha said, "I will snuff the light from your eyes and leave your body to be eaten by dogs."

"Ooo, good comeback," Tracy had to admit.

"BUT WE CAN BRING PEOPLE BACK TO LIFE, RIGHT?" shouted Irene.

Just as Cynthia began to lose the fight, perhaps to slip into oblivion, Jacquelaesha let her go, kicking her in the ribs for good measure just as she took that first big gasp of air.

"And stay away from Rubio! You don't deserve him!" Jacquelaesha said. Rubio was rubbing his left hand nervously.

"Jacquelaesha, please. I must have you." He said. And she longed for him too, but she had a lot to think about. And she needed to find Gloom.

"I'm sorry. I —" she ran away crying. There, at the edge of the castle, Gloom sat stoically.

"Well. I didn't expect to see you again." He said.

"Oh G-Gloom."

"When you spared my life, it made me realize that you could never love a man like me. I'm too broken, too dangerous. You're too pure for me Jacquelaesha, even though you've had the hard life of an outcast. Even the king recognizes your greatness. We must never be."

"No Gloom," Jacquelaesha said, "You don't understand. I love you."

"You love Rubio. He's the golden son of the lord the yellow realm, and a fine catch. Sure, they suffer in their interior design. But it's nothing like what I had to go through."

Jacquelaesha gasped. Gloom stared forlornly into the distance.

"You had to kill your parents?" she asked.

"No."

"You're not…. Under eighteen?"

"No! No," Gloom said, "No. I mean… I've just told you my terrible secret."

"That you *didn't* kill your parents?"

"Yes. Because all blues have to, or kill themselves, or suffer the pestilence, but I avoided it all. It's my darkest secret and greatest shame. No one must know, but you I can trust."

Jacquelaesha gasped. Gloom had shared with her a dark secret that was the cause of his unwavering angst, but it simultaneously made him more attractive since it turned out he didn't do any of the gross creepy things we were told his kind do at the beginning. Phew!

"Gloom. You have a hard exterior, but I can see through it." Jacquelaesha said.

Gloom glanced up at her, years of sorrow behind his eyes, the pain of his people and of all the realm's terrible curses etched into his face. "That's not the only thing that's hard," he muttered.

Then, they had sex. Because this is a book for adults. It's not *for* kids. The characters can curse and drink. And have sex. It's for adults.

Jacquelaesha was walking back to her room, futzing with her latex, when someone grabbed her from behind and put a hand over her mouth.

"This is a kidnapping!" the person announced conveniently, and evilly.

"Humph ermmerrr ump huh!" Jacquelaesha said fearfully.

"Shut up you bitch!" the kidnapper said, meanly.

"Get away from her, you bitch!" said a voice, confidently. It was Gloom!

"What are you going to doing about it?" the kidnapper said smarmily, "Bitch."

"I order you to let her go!" Gloom took his hood off (he was wearing a hood). The kidnapper gasped.

"Lord Bleaker!" he gasped, again, and let Jacquelaesha go. Now she could see that her would-be kidnapper was of the blue realm. Instead of saving her with strength or skill, Gloom had exercised the power of the state to force someone of less privileged birth to obey him. It was hot.

"Ooo, nepo *baby*," Jacquelaesha said, and thrust her hips forward with a grunt. The kidnapper dashed into the night, and Gloom pulled her into a tight embrace.

"Oh Jacquelaesha, that was too close," he shed a single tear of concern, "I recognized that man. He used to serve my father, but he was dismissed for being the worst. I can't believe he's here at the Swinging Games®."

"You don't have to protect me Gloom. I can handle myself," Jacquelaesha said, inexplicably.

"No. You can't. In fact, you shouldn't even be around me. I'm too dangerous for you. You should go back to Rubio," Gloom said, preposterously.

"I can't believe you would betray me like that!" Jacquelaesha said, against all internal and external logic.

"No, Jacquelaesha wait – !" Gloom said, but it was too late. Jacquelaesha ran crying through the night. She couldn't believe she had loved him, and yet he had betrayed her.

✟✟

Jacquelaesha woke up. It was the third day of the Games®, and King James was expected to respond to her world-shattering

33

proclamation from yesterday, deciding the fate of the entire realm in the process. She looked at her time pictometer. She was late! Ugh!

Down in the Gaming Center, the crowd was already gathered. Jacquelaesha turned heads as she entered, not that that was unusual, but she knew that this time it was because of the king thing and not her unearthly beauty.

"I'm looking at you for your unearthly beauty," Rubio clarified. He had never betrayed her, unlike certain someones. She glanced back and saw Gloom, frowning sexily under his hood.

"Jacquelaesha, you don't know that man, do you?" Rubio asked, aghast, "He's dangerous. I order you not to talk to him."

She giggled. Rubio was being so protective! Still, it was super hot how Gloom was pouting. And she was still turned on by him trauma-dumping on her the night before. Rubio had never so much as told her his most tender emotional wounds.

Suddenly, the king appeared. Silence descended over the crowd.

"Good morning," King Henry James said, "Now, in addition to the games we have a few agenda points to get through today, so I'll try to keep us on pace. First, I understand we've had several complaints that participants were unable to get their parking validated. Only licensed Swinging Games® stores are able to validate parking, so if you're asking the food vendors, or the ticket takers, you need to head to one of *five* – that's almost as many realms as there are, people – *five* official stores and ask there. Employees at the stores are aware of the situation and are happy to validate you for the previous two days. Secondly, regarding the mind-blowing moral question posed by young Jacquelaesha yesterday, I've decided to execute her."

Everyone gasped. Especially Jacquelaesha. Two guards pulled her forward, and she stood facing the stadium. She was wearing a violet and black bustier with satin ribbons that cinched her waist, and leather cups that pushed her boobs way up. Her boots were thigh high and shiny black, and her skirt had black and purple tule.

The executioner approached her. He was wearing black pants, black and red boots, and a black shirt that laced up but the laces were undone. He had a black hood that said MCR on it. He was holding…. An axe! *Electric guitar riff*

"DID ANYONE ELSE HEAR THAT" Irene shouted.

"Now, Jacquelaesha, you will die for our sins. You are too pure and we are not ready for your message. Greg, do it."

Greg raised the axe. Jacquelaesha shed a single tear. She would be… forever… an outcast….

"No!" two men shouted at once, emerging from the crowd. They stared at each other, "Jacquelaesha?"

"You! You're too dangerous for her!" Rubio shouted.

"I think Greg's too dangerous for her," Gloom said.

"Hey, you got a problem buddy?" Greg said.

"Maybe I do," said Gloom.

"Ooh, tough guy," said Greg.

"Yeah, keep talking pal," said Gloom.

"Maybe I will."

"Maybe I won't listen."

"You shouldn't."

"Good."

"I know it's good."

"Fine," Gloom walked away, then turned back, "Wait, no! No, don't execute Jacquelaesha!"

"I don't tell you how to do your job," Greg said.

"Please, King Henry James!" Rubio pleaded, "You must spare Jacquelaesha's life. I…. love her!"

Cynthia shrieked from the crowd. Rubio rubbed the fingers on his left hand nervously.

"I love her too!" Gloom proclaimed. The crowd gasped. The king gasped.

"Two noble men of the realms who are in love with the outcast," the king summed up, "they paint a portrait of this lady that is different from what I originally saw. It's really turning my screw. I wish I could sit in Washington Square to think this issue through, perhaps consult with Daisy Miller. But there's no time. You two must battle each other to win her hand… and her life."

"No!" cried Gloom.

"Oh, so it is *that* Henry James," Rubio said.

Greg pulled Jacquelaesha aside as the two men entered the arena. That intense organ music from that one Star Trek episode started playing, as the crowd cried for blood. They battled. But they were too evenly matched!

"Enough!" yelled King James. "Clearly neither of you can beat the other. Jacquelaesha: you must choose for yourself? Which side of the triangle will you pick?"

Jacquelaesha gasped. Choose? But she loved them both. Rubio for his blondness and misogynistic condescension. Gloom for his hot face and manipulative angst.

"I – I c-choose…" Jacquelaesha said, "Rubio!"

Rubio gasped! Then he dipped her and kissed her, with tongue.

"NOOOOOOOOOOOOOOOOOOOOO!!!!!!!!!!!" screamed a shrill nasty scream. It was Cynthia! She leapt from the crowd and cried, "GREG – THE AXE!" *Electric guitar riff*

"Um, ma'am, I do not know you," Greg said.

"IT HAPPENED AGAIN WHAT IS THAT," said Irene.

"Cynthia please, you're embarrassing yourself," Rubio said, nervously rubbing the third finger on his left hand. Cynthia was crying, in an ugly way. She held up her hand. Jacquelaesha noticed she had a ring on, which was gold. Odd, because orange people almost always wore orange. Now if a yellow realm person were to have a gold ring on, that would make more sense. In fact, Rubio did wear such a ring, on the finger he was now conspicuously shielding from view. In fact, the rings matched. Jacquelaesha put a hand to her chin to think. Did Cynthia and Rubio have some kind of past?

"Enough!" shouted King Henry James, "this farce has gone on long… enough. Ahem. What I mean is, I let myself be swayed by others instead of living my truth. Jacquelaesha's getting executed."

"Okie dokie," said Greg, who was standing next to a sobbing Cynthia.

"No!" Gloom shouted, "Your majesty, there's something very important that you don't understand."

"He said he was living his truth, it's toxic for you to try to convince him otherwise," said Tracy.

"Your majesty, only a violet winning the Swinging Games® can break the curse!"

Everyone gasped.

"Well didn't you break that out at the 11th hour," said Rubio.

"Perhaps! I have heard rumors, and there is the old prophecy about an outcast being the key to breaking the curse," King James said, "But even so, she is not the only violet here."

The king pointed his finger out at the crowd. *Don't pick Blag, don't pick Blag* Jacquelaesha thought. The king stopped, and commanded the person to step forward.

"You there violet, what's your name?"

"Blag."

Godammit Jacquelaesha thought.

"No!" Gloom shouted, "You still don't understand. It's not just any violet. Only Jacquelaesha, herself, solo, can break the curse."

Even though they'd done a lot already, the crowd gave an even bigger gasp.

"M-me?" Jacquelaesha stammered.

"Yes. Jacquelaesha, you don't know how special you are, or how beautiful," Gloom said, "the prophecy speaks of a violet who can capture the darkest of hearts. And…. You captured mine."

"Oh, Gloom!" Jacquelaesha cried.

"And, I'm really dark, Just to clarify." Gloom said.

"Were you gonna let me chop her head off before you told everyone that?" Greg asked.

"You really need to chill out bro," Gloom snapped.

"Deadass, I'm cool, bro," said Greg.

Suddenly, a maniacal laugh sounded over the Gaming Center. They all turned to see a gaunt blue man, dressed in dark rags and brandishing an orb. Jacquelaesha recognized that evil laugh anywhere – the man who tried to kidnap her!

"What is the meaning of this?!" demanded King James. From the orb came a beeping sound.

"CRIPES HE'S GOT A BOMB!" yelled Irene.

Everyone took one step back. And they gasped.

"Balthazar! I order you –" said Gloom, but Balthazar just laughed.

"You have no power over me anymore, sad prince," Balthazar said, "You are the ghost of the glory your ancestors once had, you hang like the dangling skin of a gluttonous man, once stuffed to the brim with fatty foods, now shriveled and starving due to his own negligence. Starving. The young children whose parents are dead. Their brother has killed them, but he does not know how to care for them. He is selfish, as are all who survive. For is it not without shedding the blood of the pig that we are fed? Is it not without the misfortune of the neighbor that we gain his land? Ah, it is so in these realms, but in the Blue we crave the death of those who love us most and whom we most love. I once was selfish. I did the deed; I let my parents bleed; let my sisters and brothers starve; but I was not prepared to go myself. My son, whom I loved most in the world, is gone, all to protect his father. Thus man's true nature was revealed to me, so I say, to you king and all the realms that there is no good end but this one. I shall be our savior! I shall spill our blood back to gods! For I am become death, destroyer of worlds, and all shall heed my vengeance with their lives!"

No one said anything after that. Jacquelaesha tried to take a step back, but tripped and fell forward (she's so clumsy), and one of the one of the daggers she kept in her boots slipped out, bounced off Greg's axe, on to Rubio's mysterious gold ring, up and off of the

King's crown, on top of Blag's thick head, and then blade first into Balthazar's eye.

"AHHHHHHHHHHH! AHHHHHHHH!" He screamed in pain, falling to ground. The blood exploded out of his head, he foamed at the mouth and died with a look of ghastly serenity.

The orb beeped.

"…. I can diffuse bombs," Blag said.

Goddamit thought Jacquelaesha.

From the ground, Cynthia stood, pointed and shouted, "GREG! NOW!"

Greg swung the axe and took off Rubio's head.

"NOOOOOOOOOOOOOO!" said Jacquelaesha.

"Yikes-olla," said King James.

"WE CAN BRING HIM BACK TO LIFE THOUGH, RIGHT, WE CAN DO THAT, I'M NOT MISREMEMBERING SOMEHOW?" Irene asked.

"God, Irene, shut up. Keep it on the D-L." Cynthia said.

"Jacquelaesha, I can't image the pain you must be feeling," Gloom said. Then, they totally made out.

"When in Rome!" Greg said to Cynthia, and then they kissed.

"I'M BORED AND BISEXUAL," said Irene, and she and Tracy made out.

"All's well that ends well!" King Henry James said, and kissed his husband. Betchya didn't see that coming, homophobes. I'm an *ally*.

"But you just had Irene and Tracy kiss," said Blag.

It's different when it's chicks, Blag. God. This is why you're uglier than Jacquelaesha.

"Come on Blag, let's make out too," Dirkard said.

"Okay but –" Blag was standing near Gloom and Jacquelaesha, totally bothering them, "Hey, excuse me. Excuse me!"

"Oh my god Blag, what is your damage?!" Jacquelaesha asked.

"So, if Gloom's secret is that he didn't kill his parents, but he's the prince of the realm, then, wouldn't everyone know that?

Because his parents are the rulers, and everyone must know how old he is. Did he secret his parents away when he turned eighteen? But then, he'd be the actual ruler of the realm, not the prince, because his parents would fake their own deaths –"

"Um, wow, you are so wrong," Gloom said, "And it's Gloomithy to you."

"- But Balthazar recognized him as the ruler, meaning everyone in the blue realm must *think* he killed his parents. Either that or he's pretending to be younger than he is, but that would be way too complicated, wouldn't it. And how did he avoid the curse anyway?"

"Wow, Blag, you're like, so obsessed with my life it's embarrassing," Jacquelaesha said. She turned to King James, "King Henry James, I've enjoyed your Swinging Games® --"

"A Good Time for the Whole Realm," the king said.

"—Yes, exactly. But now I've found something more important than winning… love."

Everyone in the crowd went *Awwwwww.*

A horse whinnied from over Balthazar and Rubio's corpses. It was Girlboss!

"Come on Gloom, let's ride!" said Jacquelaesha. They both hopped on Girlboss, and rode off into the sunset, which was sort of orange creamsicle-y.

"Well," announced King James, "I think we've all had enough. I'm ending this year's Games®, because without Jacquelaesha there really is no point. I'm sure this Games® will be legendary, so you really will want to pick up that special edition merch. Anyway, to the realm I say: see you in two years."

And with that, King Henry James Swinging Games® were over…. OR WERE THEY?!

END

"But how did Gloom avoid the blue curse? Is that and the fact that he knew about Jacquelaesha and the violets somehow related? Did he find some special info about the curse? And also, it wasn't broken –" said Blag. But no one listened to her.

Because she was ugly and annoying.

About the Author

Jacqueline Daytona has been writing all her life, and has created literally hundreds of stories from the time she was four until the present day. Not one for sports, she loves books, movies, singing, and has always been drawn to magical fantasy lands with strong female protagonists. Though she has been ostracized and called a "dork", she knows it's only because she's more intelligent and sensitive than her peers, and has channeled those feelings into her art. Natalie S. wouldn't know art if it punched her in the kidneys.

Coming Soon

Jacquelaesha 4: The Resistance Revolution

Jacquelaesha 5: Spell & Fang

Jacquelaesha 6: The Good, The Blag, and the Jacquelaesha

Jacquelaesha 7: All Glory to the Hypnohorse

Jacquelaesha 8: Jacquelaesha Onassis and the Mystery of the Magic Bullet

Praise for the Jacquelaesha Series

"I used to have no confidence. I thought that girls couldn't do ANYTHING. I had lived my entire life in a dark room and couldn't even read, but the first time I picked up a Jacquelaesha book, not only did I immediately become literate but I learned to love myself so deeply that I was able to go out, get a job, and become the first female of CEO of a military aerospace manufacturer to have contracts with the United States, Iran, North Korea, Quatar, and Vatican City."

- *Melinda H.*

"Stunning. Dripping with animal sexuality."

- *Gareth McPhoyle, editor, PCNR*

"The pillars of Göbekli Tepe are currently the oldest known site of large structures built by humankind, dating back around 12,000 years ago, as far away from Sumerian clay as Sumer is to us. And if you look closely at those carvings, you may see a horse, you may see a woman riding a horse, and that woman may have luscious black hair and clearly be hot but in a feminist way. I believe Jacquelaesha to be a primeval human story, one that touches to the very core of our species."

- *Neil deGrasse Tyson*

"I wept, for there were no worlds left for Jacquelaesha to conquer."

- *Kendra R.*

"It's good. It's very good. That's my quote, Jackie."

- *Amelia T.*

"An outcry of rage and despair against a destructive, abusive society. The poem's raw, honest language and its Hebraic-Melvillian bardic breath is the work of a thoroughly honest poet, who is also a highly competent technician… The qualities cited helped make *Howl* the manifesto of the Beat Movement and the voice of a generation."

- *The San Francisco Chronicle*

www.ingramcontent.com/pod-product-compliance
Lightning Source LLC
Chambersburg PA
CBHW032003140726
47988CB00019B/3206